I0579366

One Night
of
Moonlight

A SHORT STORY SEQUEL TO

THE MOONLIGHT PEGASUS

C. S. Johnson

For Sam—skeptic and friend, inspiration and exasperation.

For my own children, who ground me in real life even as they spur on my daydreams.

And finally, for Craig Houston and his family. We haven't met, but one day Lem will introduce us, and Krissy will be along to explain everything.

***

One night a man had a dream …

~ From "Footprints"

***

***

One Night of Moonlight

***

The sand nestled between her toes, allowing her to sink slowly into its sunlit warmth, before the chilly water came up to slosh playfully at her feet. She giggled at the strange contrast and considered her laughter a sign she was finally right where she should be: standing on the edge of Sapphira's large sea, letting the wispy waters kiss her feet while she resisted the urge to jump and leave the sandy beach behind. Despite the temptation, Terra kept still, knowing that others, her governess Kadrianne included, would say splashing around in the surf was a childish thing to do.

It was also, Terra thought with a small cringe, something her mother would probably do. And if her mother did it, Terra knew her father would likely be close behind. Her father was all that was proper when it came to dealing with the King and his court and his councilors, but the instant he was alone with his wife or his daughter, his joy was always apparent.

Well, Terra thought, most of the time, anyway. There were some startling exceptions to that, and she remembered those clearly, as though they had been etched in her mind and burned into her dreams.

"No," she said, surprised to hear her own voice reply. "Not my dreams. There are no longer any dreams for me."

She doubted they would come back, too, now that she was back on Jewel Island, visiting her father's family and once more helping with her mother's royal missions.

Terra forced the familiar pain back down inside of her. She squared her shoulders as she looked down the beachfront again. The hem of her long, white dress skimmed over the sea as she stood, still waiting, while the wind braced gently against her back. She almost wished she had changed into a shorter dress, but after arriving earlier, she could hardly wait to find some quiet time to herself. She had taken the time to throw off her shoes, even though she suspected that one of the guards, or even her best friends, Davi and Carla, would have probably picked them up.

Carla was her cousin as well as one of her friends, and both Davi and Carla were children of her parents' court. There were many days Terra could tell both of them were raised to regard the royal family, too, because while they were helpful and polite, both had been obviously crestfallen to hear she wanted some time alone.

As if three days on a ship were not enough, Terra thought. She recalled how she had played and talked and walked and did any number of things with them over the last several days. It was more than a little suffocating, even if she genuinely enjoyed her friends.

Now, she was so happy to be free, to be back on land. Terra glanced back up at the sky, with its vibrant shades of blue, stark pink, and warm yellow. It was the end of another beautiful day on Sapphira. The small planet had been cloaked in gray sunlight for years before she was born, or so the old stories went. As Terra looked up at the sky, with its multitude of colors and shades, she had a new appreciation for the tales she heard while growing up.

The stories always started at the beginning, about how the Guardian of Dreams had created the small planet of Sapphira. He had placed beauty in every inch of the earth, calling up crops and collecting animals, dividing the seas and raising up the land. He continued to give his people even more good through dreams, letting the gifted visions fall out of the sky; the people would look to him as his spirit surrounded them and permeated them, giving them life, even as he was life itself.

And then Obsidian, an evil dreamer, betrayed the Guardian by unleashing the Dark Plague. The people, suddenly unable to grasp onto the light and keep hold of it, blocked out the Spirit of Truth. The dreams of the people were no longer beautiful, and the world fell into dying darkness. The Guardian vowed to one day to send the Spirit back to the people and restore them to his celestial kingdom of Crystallon.

Terra let her eyes mist over as she glanced down at the sea. Her mother told her that she was the one who had been given the beautiful dreams, the ones of Pegasus, the form of the Spirit of Truth.

For some reason, Terra had a harder time believing this part of the story. She did not know if she actually believed it. She did not know if she *could* believe it.

A small breeze brushed by again, as if the planet wanted to prove itself more worthy of her attention. She blinked, and her gaze went once more to the horizon. It was getting close to sundown, but Terra was determined to stay where she was.

After all, she had taken care to arrive here in the first place. As much as she might have liked going back inside and forgetting about this adventure, there was a sickly feeling in her gut at the thought of it. It would seem so close to cheating.

She had to give him a full chance to keep his promise.

Then, and only then, would she have all the proof in the world she needed to let everything go completely. She could go on and live her life exactly the way she wanted to, and there would be no looking back.

It would be over, Terra thought with a grimace. Everything, everything she had ever wondered about would be settled, and she would have no reason to doubt.

Terra glanced around again before she let out a shaky sigh. *I hope he does not expect me to do this every day I am here.*

But, she thought, he would have heard I was coming, while I was with my family and friends on the ship, on our way over here. How he had found her last time?

Terra shook her head. She had to tell herself she was not making excuses. As much as she might have liked that idea, the thought of heading down to the beach every day, right before nighttime arrived, was troublesome. She had looked forward to the venture down to the beach earlier when she was on the royal ship. After sailing through the rough seas for several days, she was ready to have her feet planted on solid ground—or at least semi-solid ground. She smiled as she glanced down at her feet again, reveling in the otherworldly coarseness of the sand.

It really was a world of difference from her home.

Terra lived in the Palace in Diamond City with her parents and her uncle, and the rest of the royal court. The Table, the high plateau that housed her home, was a magnificent place of constructed beauty, one that enjoyed its harmony with nature even as it sought to defy it. The palace itself was full of examples, showing off the grandest architecture Sapphira had to offer. There were marble floors and grand gardens, many with updated rooms and new additions added over the years, especially since the great attack by her Uncle Aemon.

Terra frowned at the thought of her father's family. They were supposed to have dinner on the island while they were here; she hoped she would be able to get out of most of it. Over the years, she had always felt there was some tension between them; not bad, but not overly friendly. They had their own lives, and while they did the best they could to make them good ones, Terra had a feeling that if they were not related they would never willingly get along as friends.

Thankfully, her Aunt Cyerra, Carla's mother and her own mother's faithful friend, managed to soothe things over more often than not. She seemed to be the bridge between their worlds, and it was enough to keep their family content. They worked together on many of her mother's projects, too, she recalled, and that helped as well.

Either way, Terra decided, ultimately, it did not matter much. She preferred spending her time on the beach when she came to Jewel Island. It was the only thing she was possibly looking forward to this time.

It was only her first day on the beach of Jewel Island. Her mother, Princess Selene of Sapphira, had promised her that she would have plenty of time and opportunity to enjoy herself once they arrived. Jewel Island had lots to do; there was a small town nearby, near the main island port, and there were several sports and games and events around.

It was enough for Terra to see her mother somewhat happy again. That let her believe even more implausible things were possible, even if she remained skeptical.

But it did seem like things had changed, Terra thought. Traveling with her family on their first annual tour of the Islands in several years, the royal trek around the small collection of islands strewn along the ocean currents, had gone better than she could have hoped. So far.

She glanced back at the large house behind her, where she knew her mother and father were settling in, along with the servants. They had allowed her some time for herself, and Terra was grateful. This was the first year she had come with them since everything changed so drastically, and she did not want her parents to realize there was only one reason she had really wanted to come.

She had a promise to keep.

Or rather, a promise will be kept, she corrected herself. After all, she was not the one who made the promise. Someone else had made it to her, and she did her part to fulfill it.

She was here on the beach, after all. Just like he had asked of her.

Shira and Kuro, Sapphira's small moons, gleamed at the edge of her planet's horizon. Catching sight of their dim lighting, Terra was immediately encouraged. She still remembered that day, all too clearly, when the magic of the moonlight vanished from her life. Seeing the small remnants of sunlight barely reflecting off their mismatched faces gave her hope.

But her hope quickly faded as the temperature slipped down, and the night seemed to come more quickly. Moments, both peaceful and anxious, passed before Terra felt a surprising rush of disappointment settle inside of her stomach.

He is not going to come, she thought bitterly. She bit her lip, letting her gray eyes scan the horizon for any sign of movement.

She blinked back the rush of bitter tears when she saw a shadow moving closer from behind her. Terra sucked in her breath and held it.

Is it Lem? Is he really here?

"There you are, Terra."

In the darkening light, Terra finally recognized the figure heading toward her. It was her father. Terra's breath rushed out in frustration. "What is it, Dad?"

In the many years since Etoileon and Selene had gotten married, Terra had to wonder that her father had ever been younger than he was now. He was nearing forty, but he still stood tall and straight, with a Fighter's pride and the Guardian's confidence. Despite others' comments and thoroughly expressed concerns, he wore comfortable clothes, light and airy shirts that were just stylish enough to be fitting for the Prince consort of the planet. She glanced down and saw that he had his shoes on still; it was likely he had not been expecting her to be so far away from Jewel Island's Guest House.

She knew from the small smile on his face that he was bothered some by her wanderings, but he understood. Terra suddenly wondered if Davi had said something to a guard or his mother; she would not be surprised. She knew Kadrianne was one of her mother's former handmaidens, and now, as her governess, her fondness for rules and kindness always seemed to supersede Terra's preference for freedom.

Terra glanced around, her eyes running across the flowering foliage, seeking out any sign of her friend. When she saw a quiet rustle, followed quickly by a small patch of dark brown hair disappearing, she frowned. Davi had been watching over her. Now that her dad was with her, Terra knew he would leave.

He wouldn't want to make his mother worried, she thought, thinking of her mother's friend. Kadrianne always seemed like a worrier to her, and her son was no exception.

"What is it?" her father asked. "Do you see something?"

"It's nothing," Terra murmured, before giving him her full attention once more. As she did, she could not resist a smile. Her dad had always seemed so strong, so solid to her; he was the rock of her life, and she knew it.

"With that daydreaming look in your eyes, you're your mother's daughter," he said. "She would have said she heard a horse, if she were here."

But would she actually hear one? Terra wondered. She decided it was best to keep that question to herself.

Her mother's faith had never bothered her before Tristan. Her mother was radiant, rightly held as a beautiful lady, inside and out. She cared for her brother, the King, and cared for her family with an unrivaled love. Everyone Terra had ever met always told her what an inspiration her mother was, and how much her people admired her.

The praise her mother received was almost enough to make her nervous. She had no idea how she would live up to that, especially when the King did not seem to like her father much.

And her father was such a wonderful man.

He looked at her now, tired but still going strong after the long day. "I've come to collect you," he replied with an easy smile, the one he always saved just for her. "Your mother and I have everything situated at the house. We wanted to see if you were ready to come in for the night."

Terra glanced around the beach again. There were no other shadows walking along the beach, making their way to her. "I don't want to go in just yet," she whispered.

"What are you waiting for?" Etoileon asked.

Terra kept her face hidden from him as she glanced across the seascape in front of her. The air was so crisp and salty, the warmth of it so alive and potent. The water still lapped at her feet, simultaneously tender and quiet, like a mother's midnight lullaby.

She felt her father come up behind her, and she hesitated to let him come close. Terra did not want to admit that no matter how close they were, and no matter how much he loved her or she loved him, there was a distance between the two of them.

"You know, your mother was really happy you decided to come," Etoileon remarked carefully. "She was worried you would not want to come here again."

Terra bristled. He knew what she was thinking. He put his hand on her shoulder, and she could not stop a flinch. But there was no moving away from him.

"I miss him, too," he said quietly.

"You don't miss him as much as I do," Terra insisted, unable to stop herself from angrily lashing out. "And that's not even the worst part, you know. I miss you and mom, too. You're not the same since Tristan died."

Etoileon felt the sting of unwelcome surprise as he looked down at his daughter. She was nearly a teenager, he thought, profoundly awed by the young woman she was becoming. Ever since she was born, he had wondered throughout the years how bright and brilliant she would shine. Just like her mother, she had a caring heart and a kind smile.

But unlike Selene, she had been brought up in a world where everything was happy and perfect. It was only when Tristan passed that the world suddenly turned into a frightening place, one that was somehow even worse because of all the brightness before. Etoileon thought about how Terra had changed since that day, four years ago.

"Your brother is in a better place," he told her quietly. "I know how you feel. I know it is terrible to feel his loss."

"How do you know?" Terra asked. "How do you know for sure?"

"I've seen Pegasus," Etoileon reminded her. "Adamas is real, Terra. He healed me before, and he saved your mother. And many others have seen him, too."

What did that matter to her? Terra had to wonder. Other people were like her, maybe, but she was not them, and they were not her. Maybe not all of them had seen how life had been good and grand, and then everything had been turned upside down.

"Well, *I* haven't seen him," Terra scoffed. She almost rolled her eyes at the mention of her parents' dream god. The idea that somehow a man could transform into a flying horse and fly through people's dreams was silly. Especially to her.

Etoileon tried again. "I've met him. I know him. And he knows your mother. Remember all the stories she used to tell you about him?"

"They could be just stories," Terra insisted. She folded her arms across her chest defiantly. "Just like all the stories you told me about how when Tristan came, he would play with me and grow up with me, and I would get to protect him and … "

Her voice trailed off as her tears once more cluttered her vision. Her father knelt down before her, the seawater rushing up and running over his legs, pulling him deeper into the sand as it had tugged on Terra earlier.

Terra ignored him and cleared her throat, trying to force herself back to her usual self.

This is Lem's fault, she thought. If she had not been so anxious to see if he would keep his promise, she would have never even thought about all of this again.

"Hey," Etoileon said. He cupped her chin tenderly. "It is not your fault that he died. The doctors told us that he had been slowly dying inside your mother for weeks."

"I was supposed to protect him. But I couldn't," Terra said, barely realizing she was saying the words aloud. They had been silently tucked away inside her heart for many years now, and the last person she wanted to tell them to was her father.

She squeezed her eyes shut again, before she finally allowed herself to look into her father's matching gray eyes. She could see the small specks of silver in them, just like her mother had always mentioned before. The small amount of moonlight seemed all the brighter in her father's eyes.

He wrapped his arm around her. "I couldn't protect him, either," he whispered. "I know you feel like a failure as a sister. I know your pain, as his father."

Terra bit her lip again, this time not only to push back her tears, but to keep any words from coming out.

She had known of her father's pain, having witnessed it for the past several years in unexpected moments, watching him as he saw her mother's bright cheerfulness sobered by inconsistent bouts of depression.

Etoileon gathered her to him, pulling her up against his heart as he had done all her life. Even though she was twelve years of age, Terra was still able to rest her head on his shoulders and feel the familiar comfort he offered. Despite her inner turmoil, Terra could not resist another smile. He was trying so hard to get her to feel better, she realized.

Like she had countless times before, she tucked her pain away, with a sense of duty along with a sense of relief.

"If you want, we can go and see his grave tomorrow," Etoileon promised her, ruffling her brown locks affectionately. "You and I, and your mother, too."

"No," Terra objected. "I don't want to go with Mom."

"She's gotten much better lately," Etoileon remarked quietly. "Why do you think she agreed to come out here again?"

"I know she has her mission work," Terra grumbled. "And I know you like to tag along because it's Mom, and also your brother and his family are out here. You don't like to see him and his work go unaccounted for in the Kingdom, even if it's good."

Etoileon pursed his lips. "True, Aemon has never been a complete pleasure to deal with, given our rather unpleasant history. But we have gotten better in the last ten years or so," he said with a small laugh. "You're becoming very observant, aren't you?"

"You're the one who told me that a Fighter always has to be observant of the smallest things," Terra snorted.

Etoileon took her hand. "You're also very smart," he said. "Come on, Terra. I know your mother will be worried if we're not back soon. And she will not be the only one."

Terra groaned. "I figured Davi was the one who told on me. Kadrianne must have told him to keep tabs on me."

"Actually, it was both Davi and Carla who told me where you were," Etoileon said. "So you can blame them both. Kadrianne is helping your mother at the moment."

"Ugh."

Etoileon tightened his grip on her. "They're your best friends, my darling," he said. "They are worried for you, too, just as your mother and I have been."

"You don't need to worry about me," Terra insisted.

"We love you," he replied. "And we have all been through an especially hard time. Your mother was a lot like you when I first met her, you know."

"You've told me."

"She used to have a hard time with sadness, too," Etoileon continued. There was a catch in his throat as he added, "When I first met her, she was very lonely. With Tristan's passing, I've seen some of it come back, and come back stronger than either of us could have ever thought. But we are getting through it. Sometimes there is nothing we can do but worry, it seems. Even if it's not really a good idea."

"You're the one who taught me that it is foolish and impractical to worry about what might be," Terra said.

"Being a Fighter, Terra, is a job. There is no job that is the same as living as a human. There are many, many differences between those two things."

Terra scrunched up her face. Her father was treating her like such a child. She was glad they were walking up the stairs to the Guest House.

It was a nice home, she thought, as she saw the last of the sunshine slip below the sea. The wooden structure was clearly worn in some areas, but it had been a home to Jewel Island's many prominent leaders. In the last several years, the leader of Jewel Island had made a bid to build a new residence on the other side of the island, so the Guest

House had been prepared as a special place for important guests to come.

It was here on Jewel Island that Her Highness, the crown princess of Sapphira, Princess Selene, had been visiting when the tragedy happened.

Terra closed her eyes against the rush of images that began running through her mind. She tried to break free from her father, but he only held on more tightly, as if he knew what she was going through.

Terra resisted as much as she could, but the moment she caught sight of her mother, looking out of the window at the top of the turret, Terra could no longer fight back the haunting memories.

***

Her mother had always been beautiful, but at six months pregnant with her brother, Terra, at seven years old, found a new level of awe as she watched her mother move around the Guest House. Her mother's hair, a pretty dark blonde, blew gracefully in the salty wind, adding a layer of fun to all her movements.

Together, the two of them would make their lunch and carry it up the stairs, Selene moving slowly. The tower was a favorite place for them, as they were able to see far off into the distance.

They settled into the window seat and began to eat. "This is such a nice place," Selene said, as she patted her bulging belly. "I think the baby likes it, too. He's asleep right now and seems very peaceful."

"That's because you're moving so much, Mommy," Terra said. "You're rocking him to sleep."

"You're so clever, my sweet princess," Selene replied, giving her daughter a pat on the head. "You've been listening well to the doctor."

Terra placed her hand over her mother's belly. The frilly folds of her mother's dress were soft and smooth, and she willingly pressed into the fabric, trying to feel where her brother was.

"Ooh, careful," Selene murmured. "Not too hard, Terra. We wouldn't want him to wake up while he's sleeping."

"Do you think he's having some good dreams?"

Selene gave her a bright smile. "Of course," she said. "It's part of our family. You have good dreams, too, don't you, Terra?"

Terra nodded as her mother began to move around. "I can't wait to have him come," Terra said. "I wish he would come soon."

"It won't be too long now," Selene said, "although I would be the first one to agree. Carrying a baby in your belly is not the most comfortable situation."

She rubbed her stomach again, letting herself feel the quiet satisfaction of life inside of her. Terra watched as she leaned against the tower's window seat, letting herself watch the scene before her.

"Where's Daddy?" Terra asked.

"He went down to the beach," Selene said, nodding out into the distance. Terra turned her gaze toward the familiar figure of her father. She knew it was him immediately. He was running without a shirt on, and there were patches of scars on his back, remnants from the attack on the Royal Palace decades before. In the bright daylight, they shimmered with a profound purity that Terra loved to watch. She was awed by her father and his strength, but even more so at his deeds. Her mother would tell her the stories of the surprise attack on the Royal Palace. Terra was amazed that, even as much time had passed, she was able to come to Jewel Island with her family, and they were able to work together to make the world a better place.

"You can see him out there, with Ronal close behind him."

"Ronal?"

"Oh, Carla's father." Terra watched her mother's gaze. She almost giggled; Selene was transfixed by the sight of her husband, and Terra was old enough to know that her mother, after all their years of marriage, still longed for his company.

"Oh, right."

"I think I can see her, playing near them," Selene said, craning her neck to see just beyond her vision. "I think Davi's out there, too. Kadrianne will not be happy."

"She does seem overprotective of him." Terra smiled. "That's why Davi was so funny today. He told me he wants to be a Fighter when he grows up, so he can protect me."

"What is funny about that?" Selene asked.

"His mom would be too worried for that to happen," Terra said. "Besides, Daddy's my protector. I don't need a protector while Daddy's around."

Selene grinned. "I know exactly what you mean." She turned her attention back to Etoileon, and sighed softly as she soothingly rubbed her belly. "If you would like, maybe we can go down and join him after lunch."

Terra's eyes lit up. "Okay!"

But they would never make it down to the beach.

***

Terra did not want to recall the following hours. Her mother, walking out of the house, collapsed in unexpected and sudden pain.

Terra did not like to think of how terrified she had been, seeing her beautiful mother fall to the ground, practically dead to the world. She had hurried to find her father, while other guards and servants came to stay with Selene.

Terra especially did not like to think of how she had wished for the baby to come early, and how her wish had been fulfilled. As her mother cried and screamed and sobbed, her father—her strong, valiant, invincible father—broke down, as though some part of him had died.

Maybe that was what happened, Terra reasoned. She had felt that way herself, hadn't she?

Tristan was born just hours later, in the early part of the evening. He had just experienced the first and only sunset of his life before he quietly slipped away from them.

He was too small and too delicate, and too good for this world, her mother said.

Terra was only eight years old then. But she knew she had grown up that day. She knew that night, the night her brother died, and he took the beauty of the moonlight along with him.

And, she knew, there was no going back.

***

That was part of the reason she had been hesitant to come back to this place. She glanced around at her room. It was airy and open, and the windows allowed for the taste of the nearby sea to slip in and out at the whim of the breeze. She sat on her bed, with its comfy sheets and fluffy pillows, all designed especially for her use and enjoyment.

"But Lem made it worse," she said aloud.

She thought of that day again. After the horrifying loss of her brother, and her parents as well, Terra had run to the beach to get away, to wish herself to die since she had wanted so badly for her brother to come.

She was at the edge of the water, not much different than she had been earlier, when *he* came.

***

The day her brother was lost, Terra felt the burn of unrelenting tears as she ran down to the beach. She felt her feet scrap against some rocks, and the bite of the sand as it mixed with her blood, but she kept running toward the sea.

Her most beautiful dreams had always been near the sea, she thought bitterly. So it was to the sea she ran for comfort.

Terra did not want to think of dreams that day. She had always listened with awe as her mother—her bright, beautiful mother—told her of stories of Pegasus, the Spirit of Truth who had come down to Sapphira through her dreams. She told Terra of Pegasus, of his human form, and Adamas, and how he had gathered all of the Dark Plague to him, and sealed it away in the sky with his blood.

Terra had often longed to dream of Pegasus, so much so that she convinced herself, and others, that she had dreamed of Pegasus often enough.

But that stopped, too, after Tristan.

Pegasus was always so powerful, Terra thought. Why did he let her brother die? Did he not love her mother enough? And if Pegasus didn't love her mother enough to save Tristan, what hope could Terra possibly have that he would love her, too?

She had always believed her mother about Pegasus, about the Guardian of Dreams, and about Adamas. But after Tristan died, she no longer thought it was true. How could it be true? It was too terrible to be true.

That was the day, Terra thought, that moonlight disappeared from her life, and there was nothing else left to believe in, other than stark nothingness. The sunlight even seemed to dim, fading into a grayish glow in Sapphira's open skies.

After running away from her grieving family, the ocean waves washed over her bare feet. Terra did not look back at the Guest House. She already knew where everyone was. After seeing Tristan's passing, her mother fell into despair, and her father followed her. She had peeked into their bedroom before running away; her father held onto her mother, wrapping her in his arms, as they both cried over each other, their dead son cradled between them.

There was no one who was looking for her, Terra thought. She waded out into the water some more. Would they miss her, too, if she never came back? If she, like her brother before her, made her way into eternal sleep?

She had always wanted a brother, or a sister. Terra had grown up watching King Dorian as he cared for Selene. She'd witnessed his playful teasing, his loving protectiveness, and his open adoration for her mother. When her mother told her that, after long days and years of waiting, she would get a sibling, Terra had been so excited.

Her hand reached out into the waters, pulling her further into the surf. She wondered if the waves could take her out the edge of her world, letting her glimpse at her brother on the other side of the eternal plane.

"The mermaids might be calling you, Princess," a voice said from behind her. "But it's the human voices that will wake you, and you will drown if you're not careful."

Terra turned and saw a small boy, no older than her, approaching her from behind. He was strange, she thought. He had crystal-colored eyes, and his hair was the lightest blonde she had ever seen, so much that it looked white in the early morning hours.

"Who are you?" she asked.

"My name is Lemuel," he said. "But you can call me Lem. I live around here, from time to time."

"I've never seen you before."

He gave her an easy smile, one that was strangely calming, even though a warning flashed through her. "That doesn't mean I wasn't here before you," he said. "And that doesn't mean that I won't be here when you come back."

Terra frowned. "You just told me not to go."

"Yes. I told you not to go into the sea like that," Lem said. "It offers a false hope for many, just like many other things."

"Like Pegasus?" Terra said, wrinkling her nose.

"Who said anything about Pegasus?" Lem asked.

"He didn't save my brother," Terra said. "I don't want to be in a world where he could have saved him, and he didn't. And he hurt my mother, and my father because of that, too. What kind of all-powerful being does that?"

"The Dark Plague might have been defeated," Lem said, "but there are still things in this world that cause us to suffer."

"Exactly!" Terra rounded on him. "And it is terrible that my mother should be among them."

"Your mother is very nice," Lem agreed. "She is the one who comes here every year to visit with the orphaned children, to feed the widows, and to see to new construction or other projects. I've seen her around the different parts of the island."

"Yes," Terra said, nodding her head. "All she wanted was another baby. She told me that she had all sorts of trouble getting me, you know. And now she's lost my brother, Tristan."

Lem came up to her and took her hand. "I'm sorry for your loss, too, Princess."

Terra stepped away from him suddenly, disturbed by his closeness, but he did not let go of her hand. "How do you know me?" she asked. "I didn't tell you who I was."

Lem's enigmatic eyes twinkled. "Everyone knows you, Princess Terra," he said. "You have the beauty of your mother and the strength of your father. But I also know that you have your own heart. I can see it in your eyes."

"I have my father's eyes," Terra shot back. *Who is this strange boy? Why is me making me feel so … strange?*

He kept her hand firm. "Come walk with me," he said. "I know you are sad, but I can help you, if you let me. And if you trust me."

"How can you help me?" Terra asked. "It's not like you have the power to bring my brother back to life, or take away my parents' sadness."

"No, and I would not dream of trying," he said. "There are some on this Island who, to gain your trust, might say that."

"There are people who can bring my brother back?" Terra asked. "Where? Why didn't my parents send for them?"

"Because they are evil," Lem said. There was no room for doubt in his voice. "They are the Demon Chasers, and they seek to release Obsidian from his celestial prison. They hide from the Light with their own blood sacrifices, trying to gather what is left of Obsidian's power."

"Could he bring my brother back? I mean, if Pegasus can't—"

"Obsidian cannot truly bring him back," Lem said. "His followers will lure you in with their lies like that."

"Well, then how would you help me?" Terra asked. "If they can't do it, not really, and Pegasus won't, then what power do you have that would ever help me?"

"I can be your brother from now on."

Instantly, vehemently, Terra jerked away from him. "No," she spat. "No, you can't be. You dishonor my brother when you say things like that. Only he can be my brother."

"A brother can be more than blood," Lem told her. "Why not let me show you?"

"No." Terra frowned. "I'm going home now."

Between staying there and listening to a stranger tell her he could replace her brother, and going home to where she no longer had a home left, Terra knew it was smarter to venture back the way she came.

As she walked away, Lem called out to her, "I'll be here when you decide you want to come back to the beach, Princess," he said. "That's a promise. See if I don't keep it."

Terra did not want to hear him, but she did. That was why, four years later, she decided to come back to the beach again. And while she no longer dreamed, there were several times when she would wake up and wonder if he was still there, waiting for her to come back.

***

"Catch it, Terra, come on!" Carla called out to her from across the grassy field, the one close by the orphanage where Selene was working that afternoon.

It was the next day, and already the peace of arriving on land was interrupted by the royal schedule. The sun was in the middle of the sky, shining unapologetically down on her, as if the darkness of her mood was asking for some kind of compensation.

They made several stops in the morning, making their rounds at the local markets, meeting with their old friends, and seeing to the various houses and hostels. They were finishing up in the afternoon at Jewel Island's orphanage, the one her mother founded in the years before Terra was born.

Terra grumbled to herself as she looked around the campus. It was large and spacious, with plenty of room for play and open air. She was in the enclosed garden in the back, while her mother worked inside with Cyerra, Carla's mother, by her side.

All Terra wanted to do was go back to the Guest House. She had slept poorly, and she knew it was showing as Carla and Davi were trying to get a game of ball started with her help.

More accurately, without her help, Terra thought. She slumped over and grabbed the small ball, before tossing it out to the far side where Carla waited impatiently. Terra could see her friend was nearly bouncing with energy, her long hair tied back from her pretty face.

Davi came up beside her. "Don't you want to play, Terra?" he asked. "You love this game."

"I'm allowed to change my mind about things," Terra retorted. She sat down where she was and began picking at the different blades of grass.

She sighed and glanced around. She was surprised to see a strange-looking man was staring at her from across the way. From where she was, his face was slightly obscured by the hedges around the orphanage. He seemed to leer at her, and she quickly turned away.

That's weird. She shivered.

"Are you feeling well?" Davi asked, clearly hesitant.

He always seemed so nervous around her, Terra thought, irritated. She glanced back at where the man had been, and she was more than glad to see he was gone.

"Terra?" Davi's voice was patient as he tried once more to gain her attention.

Terra glared up at him. Davi was closer to her in age than Carla was, but it always seemed like Carla was the older one. Carla could easily, confidently, round up twelve to twenty children and start up a successful game of catch. That usually meant Davi was stuck catering to their mopey princess.

"I'm fine," Terra told Davi. "There's no need to worry. Just go and play with your sister. I'll be fine over here."

Davi did not turn away from her. "I was hoping you would join us," he said carefully. "We haven't played together for a while."

"We were on that ship for a few days. And besides that, we almost always see each other at the Royal Palace. So what if we don't play together?" Terra asked. "I don't want to play. If you want to, then go ahead. It's not like you have to sit here with me while the others do."

But when he did sit beside her a moment later, she huffed disdainfully.

"Why are you upset with me?" Davi asked.

His insistence was making her nervous, truth be told, but she did not want to tell him that. She decided to go with the less harmful answer. "Because," Terra said, "you were the one who followed me out to the beach last night."

That was probably why Lem did not come, Terra realized. She was being watched, first by Davi and then by her father, and probably any number of palace guards, too. Lem probably saw them and thought he would have been perceived as an attacker or something.

There was also the fact that the Guest House residents were the ones who had access to that small part of the beach. Who else would be there, except for someone who was lost, or someone who was there to harm her?

And, Terra thought, with a little bit of discomfort, Lem had been very polite to her, despite his offer to be her new brother. He had come to her before without anyone around. He would not have wanted to interrupt her time with anyone else, right?

"I'm sorry," Davi said, interrupting her thoughts about Lem. "I just didn't think it was a good idea to go out. I overheard Prince Etoileon say that there were rumors of Demon Chasers around here again. He was with your uncle, Aemon, when he said it, so I don't think he was lying."

Terra frowned. "Demon Chasers?"

"The people who want to free Obsidian's power from the Guardian's protection," Davi said, and for a moment, at his sincerity, Terra had to remember that she no longer believed in the fairy tale of her childhood.

Terra knew little of Obsidian's story, and what she did know was that he was the one who was evil, the one who was to be stopped in all of the mythic tales. He was the one who had poisoned Sapphira with the Dark Plague.

"I wonder why my dad didn't mention it to me," Terra said, thinking of how her father had come to get her the previous night. "I might have considered saying something if I had known."

"No you wouldn't have," Davi said. He gave her a shy smile. "Not you, Terra. There's nothing that you're afraid of."

She was taken aback by his admission, even as she realized it was true. After her brother died, and seeing how her mother was thrown into a deep, lasting depression for years, while her father felt the sting of failure every time he looked at her, Terra doubted there was anything worse she could fear.

"You would have just ignored it," Davi continued. "My mother said that you're reckless, just like both of your parents."

"Better than being a coward, like some people I know," Terra snapped.

Immediately, watching him blanch and then blush, Terra felt the sting of her own venom. Davi quickly stood up and walked away, and as mean and pointed as she had been, Terra could not help but think that he didn't need to go and prove her right.

She frowned at him as he walked away, too ashamed to admit she should go and apologize.

There was no need for him to make her decisions for her, right? There was no need for him to go and tell on her every time she made a movement, was there? Terra was not sure.

Davi glanced back at her when Carla came up to him, and Terra saw Carla scowl at her. Seeing the angry look on her friend's face, she had a feeling Carla would be having a talk with her later.

"Terra," Selene called out from a nearby window. "Come in here and help me."

Terra was almost relieved her mother was calling her away from her friends. But when she came to see her mother, she almost turned around.

Her mother was inside with the babies, children who had been left at the orphanage by their mothers; they could have also been children who had lost their mothers. As Terra entered the room, she saw Selene held a small baby in her hands, with a soft tuff of reddish hair.

Terra could not stop herself from thinking of Tristan, seeing the baby's sleepy eyes. She glanced up at her mother, whose own eyes were blurry with shadows, and she knew her mother was likely thinking of Tristan, too.

She has her depressed eyes again.

Terra knew every speckle in her mother's eyes, and she could trace them all like constellations according to her mother's moods. She saw the resigned sadness inside of them, but since she was there, she knew it was better that she stay.

"What is it, Mom?" she asked.

"This is Kyrigan," Selene said. "I was going to rock him for a while, but the headmistress needs a hand in the classroom she's setting up. I thought you might like to help her instead?"

"Sure. If you don't want me to take the baby instead."

"I can take care of him," Selene assured her.

Terra nodded and then hurried out of the room, before her mother could say anything else, or she could see anything else.

Why does she torture herself like this? Terra wondered. She knew that her mother had a lot of charity projects, and she loved to take care of the poor and lonely. But why did she bother with this one, or any of the ones that involved babies and children? It seemed to Terra that her mother was only making herself more upset.

After all, Terra thought, that was the reason that her parents had decided not to have any more children.

***

By the end of the day, Terra had a little more understanding of her mother's choices. When she was finished helping in the classroom, plenty of the smaller children came in to play and work. She had a few of them climbing on her, trying to hug her, trying to feel her skin. She giggled as some of them ran their tiny fingers over her. She knew that as a royal, she had an unmistakable glow to her skin that, even in the sunshine on the Islanders' home, did not disappear entirely.

When Selene and the rest of her crew were ready to go, Terra found her way back to her mother's side. She watched as her mother gave Kyrigan a sweet kiss good-bye, and she felt a new sense of pride in her mother.

Her mother was able to see through her own pain to help others handle theirs. While Terra did not like to see her mother swamped with sadness, she decided that she could be brave and try to find Lem once more.

Maybe he was busy, she thought. *Maybe he deserves another chance.*

Or maybe, she thought, she just wanted to give him one.

***

Terra headed out of the Guest House quietly. This time, she had excused herself from dinner, with the promise that she would attend the next one. Aemon had come with his family, and while the Guest House was certainly luxurious, it was much smaller than the Royal Palace back in Diamond City. With Aemon's own two children and his wife, there were twice as many distractions as usual.

Terra waited until one of her cousins dropped a plate full of food onto the floor before she made her exit. She quickly slid down the hall, and tucked herself into one of the smaller closets around the back halls to wait. If she was going to do this, she knew she would have to wait a while. And Terra was determined to do just that.

Some hours later, she heard her parents make their way to their room, and she nearly gagged as she heard their soft kisses and sweet murmurings to each other. Terra loved her parents, and she even liked that they were always so good to each other. She just decided that she hated physically seeing it, especially when there were plenty of other people around and they looked at each other like there was no one else in the world.

When the hallway outside the closet had been silent for some time, Terra eased her way out of the door, not even shutting it completely, for fear the old hinges would squeak in protest.

She tiptoed down the hall and then made a quick break for the door.

Just as she reached it, she heard a voice say, "Am I supposed to ask you where you're going? Or would that be too cowardly of me?"

Terra grimaced at the sound of Davi's voice. She turned around, and there he was.

She almost yelped in surprise, but she managed to keep her shriek in her mouth. Kadrianne's son was nothing like his mother. With his tall stature, Terra knew that the other mothers of the royal court were already betting he would be over six feet tall. He was only a few months older than her, having just turned thirteen, and he was getting pretty close to securing that bet. They had known each other their entire lives, and now that she was starting to grow up, she hated that he was able to remember her in her youth.

His voice was even starting to get deeper, she suddenly realized, briefly distracted. She was about to apologize for her earlier remark when he started talking again.

"Well?" he asked. "Should I go get your father? Or maybe my mother?"

At his indignation, she lost her compassion. Terra frowned. "Well, it's not like you want to come with me, right?" she scoffed.

"Fine," Davi said. He waved his hand toward the door. "Where are we going?"

Before she could stop him, he breezed through the door.

"Come on, stop," Terra moaned as she followed him. "I was just kidding, Davi. Go back inside and leave me alone for a while. I'm not going far, and I won't be long."

"You sure like to be alone a lot," Davi said. "And don't try to talk to me about not belonging. I know where you belong. You belong here, with your family and friends."

Terra stumbled at his words, confused and then surprised. She decided to ignore the last part. He might have thought she meant that she didn't belong here, but it was still disconcerting to hear his words. She had not meant that, anyway.

"So what if I want to be alone?" Terra wrinkled her nose. "This is not a happy place for me, or my family. I lost a brother here, and much more besides."

"You still have much to be grateful for," Davi pointed out.

"I can still mourn for what I've lost," Terra shot back. She blinked as she realized he was walking out toward the beach. "Why are you going this way?" she asked, relieved to have a chance to change the subject.

"You want to go to the beach, don't you?" The low sun in the far-off horizon blinked against the blue-green in his eyes. She never realized it before, but he had eyes that matched the sea. In the low lighting, his eyes were almost like a small bay itself, a place of shelter and security for those who had traveled through many storms.

She did not realize she was staring until he repeated his question.

Seeing no comforting alternative, Terra decided to tell the truth. "Yes," she said.

"Why do you want to go there?" Davi asked. "I know we had a few days on the boat, but there's not much that exciting about it. Even at the palace, we can travel to some of the nearby towns on the Continent and swim and play in the beaches there."

"It's different here," Terra said. She did not want to tell Davi about Lem; she had a feeling that he would be upset, for some reason, and worse, she thought he might feel compelled to be her chaperone if she told him.

"It's not much different here."

"It is for me."

"Is it because you came here when you were sad, when Tristan … I mean, all those years ago, after everything?"

"What are you talking about?" Terra asked. She stopped just as they stepped onto the sandy path down to the beachfront.

"I saw you," he said. "I was here, too, remember? Your dad and my dad came here with your mom. Your mom came with charity work and your dad came to—"

"To check on Uncle Aemon," Terra finished. It was strange to remember that visit differently than she usually did. "I remember."

For years following her parents' marriage, Terra knew there was still a small pocket of resistance, particularly out among the Islanders. Many of them that she had visited were hostile to her family at first, even her mother. But Selene, in her own soft and generous way, had managed to face them and win them over with her kindness. While her brother ruled from the top of the Table, Princess Selene was his counterpart, and she was adored around the world.

"Yes, so I was here, too," Davi said. "When you went to go get your dad off the beach when your mom started hurting, I stayed behind with her and held her hand."

"You did?" Terra asked.

"Yes. I … I prayed with her," he said. "She fainted initially, you probably remember, but when she came to a moment later, she said she was in a lot of pain. She was clearly pretty afraid. She calmed down some when I prayed. So I did."

"Is that why you believe all those stories of Pegasus even though you've never seen him?" Terra asked.

"I have seen him," Davi said. "I know he's real. Don't you?"

Terra began to walk again, this time her steps less sure than they had been before. "You know how I feel about this sort of thing, Davi," she said quietly.

"I know," he said. "But I want to hear what you think."

Terra thought about Lem again. She had been lost and alone, and he had shown up out of practically nowhere, offering to take the place of her brother. She thought about how strange he was, how she did not really even know him, but she clung to that memory like it was a lifeline.

Maybe what she thought was real wasn't true, and maybe what she thought was true, wasn't. If she knew there were things in life that could be wrong, did that not mean that some things could be right, too?

"I don't know what to think," Terra finally admitted to Davi. She sighed. "I suppose that is part of the reason I wanted to come out here."

"To figure out what to think?"

"No," she said. "That's not it."

"What is it then?" he asked, slowing his pace some, as they came to the water's foaming edge.

"I guess … I guess it's going to sound a little unusual."

Davi grinned at her. "There's nothing about you that isn't," he said. "Usually."

"Like how I can beat you in Fighter training?" Terra asked, giggling at the memory.

"It was just a couple of times, Terra." Davi rolled his eyes now. "You managed to surprise me."

"That's not as hard to do as it sounds, then, is it?" Terra grinned.

"It's harder than you think," Davi replied. "I know you very well, and I've helped watch over you since we were younger."

"Being my friend is hardly the same thing as being a bodyguard," Terra huffed.

"One day I'll prove it to you," he promised.

"Speaking of promises … " Terra looked out to where Shira and Kuro were just moving up onto the cloudy horizon once more. "That's why I wanted to come here."

"You made a promise to come?"

"No," Terra said, shaking her head. "Someone made a promise to me."

Terra told Davi about how she had met Lem, and how she was still curious to see if he would come back. She felt better about telling him the story—it was a relief to be telling the story to someone after keeping it to herself for so long—but when she saw the disapproving look on his face, she began to wonder if her earlier regret had pushed her into sharing too much.

"What?" she asked, crossing her arms over her chest as she glared at him.

"I don't know if I should tell you," he said, hesitating.

Again! Again with the hesitating … Terra scowled. "Just tell me. At this point, I'm going to be angry with you either way, so it will be better for the both of us if you let me know why I should be angry with you."

"That's not fair, Terra."

"Just skip the whining and tell me."

"Fine." He shook his head. "Terra … there was no one with you that night."

"What?" Terra nearly laughed. "I saw someone. I saw a boy, who came up to me, and talked with me. I saw him."

"You can't prove it," Davi pointed out. "All you know is that he said he'd promise to come back when you did. I didn't see him then, Terra. And I don't see him now."

"You didn't see him?" Terra repeated. "Were you spying on me or something?"

"I was trying to protect you," he insisted. "So after your dad came back to help your mother, I made sure that I kept track of you. My mother can verify that, if you don't believe me. It wasn't that many years ago. She will remember that night as much as you do."

Terra's brow creased in anger. "I'm not going to talk to your mother about that," she huffed. "You're lying. I refuse to dignify that with any response."

"You're already responding," Davi said with an angry tone. "And that's just like you, too, Terra. You don't want to do anything that doesn't automatically line up with your own beliefs."

"That's not true!"

"It is, too. I just told you I was watching you that night, as you went down to the beach. It's how I know that you wanted to come here tonight. I didn't see a boy come up to you, much less talk to you, and there's nothing you can do to prove it."

"I saw it!" Terra insisted. "I am the proof!"

"Well, I've seen Pegasus," Davi said. "But I'm not enough proof for you. Nor is your mother, or father, or any number of people."

"There's too much suffering in the world," Terra argued, ignoring the fact he was right. "What are you and my family members against a whole world of darkness? Even Pegasus died to protect this world."

"But he came back," Davi said. "He came back. He defeated it by dying with it, and it died. But people are still able to choose darkness. You know that there have been Demon Chasers spotted around here, Terra. Shouldn't they be proof that Pegasus' power is real, too, in many ways?"

"You know what? I don't want to talk to you anymore," Terra said, as she shoved him away from her. She turned on her heel, less than gracefully due to the sand, and walked away from him.

***

Davi watched her leave with a sad look on his face. He did not know if he was more upset with her or himself.

His heart felt hollow. Terra had been his close friend for many years, even before she had lost her brother. As he watched her walk away from him, he clenched his fists together, angry that he had pushed her. He only ever wanted to be with her, to hold her hand and keep her close.

He was not blind. He knew how she felt about him, about how they were just friends, and barely even that some days. Davi never wanted to wonder if she did think of him as a brother, almost, because it would have been too painful for her.

For several long moments, he stood there, right where she had left him, watching as the tides gradually came in, washing away the footprints in the sand, the ones she had left behind.

"Please, Adamas," he whispered. "Please help her heart to heal. I know she's not like this, usually. I know she has been so badly hurt, and she can't handle it alone."

He watched as the waves rolled away once more, back into the sea, before he heard a horse neighing in the distance. At once, Davi whirled around, looking for the source of the sound. When he saw nothing, he glanced back at the wet sand.

And then he saw it—there were two sets of footprints in the sand. The ones Terra had left behind, and a new set beside hers.

Pegasus.

Davi's eyes widened in happy surprise. It was just like the story Princess Selene had spoken of before, about how he come to her in a dream, as she walked along the beach.

Davi grinned and cheered to himself. *I have to show Terra,* he thought excitedly. Surely then she would believe him about Pegasus now.

"Terra!" he called out.

She did not seem to be able to hear him for all the waves.

He cupped his hands up to his mouth and took a deep breath, ready to call out to her once more. But before he could, all of a sudden someone grabbed at him from behind.

***

Terra heard a sound on the horizon behind her. She turned, letting her gaze go back toward Davi, hoping he was not trying to follow her. She thought of warning him not to do that when she realized he was being attacked.

"Davi!" Terra gasped in shock as she watched three shadowy figures, fighting and clawing at him, trying to grasp onto him.

Before she could tell herself to run, she was running.

"Hey," she cried out to the strange, cloaked figures. "Let him go!"

Terra knew from her Fighter's training she had to go and help. Davi, for all he was a proficient student, was outnumbered. Terra watched, horrified, as one of the shady figures slammed him down into the sand.

Terra clenched her fists, ready to fight. She lashed out as soon as she was in range. "Augh!" she cried, as she hit her mark.

The figure who had hit Davi groaned and tumbled to the ground. Terra could see his darkened eyes were a terrifying bloodshot red.

"Grab her, too," the man ordered, and Terra, at the rush of defeating her first official foe in battle, immediately prepared to fight off the next two.

Davi rolled to his feet beside her. "I've got your back," he told her, as they had done before in their Fighters' classes.

Terra nodded and jabbed forward, striking the other shade. "Who are you?" Terra demanded, as she watched her new target stumble.

"I am Mylan, of the Order of the Four Points," the leader said, as he stood up and dusted himself off. "I serve Obsidian, and the remnant of his power that is hidden in the darkest part of the human heart."

Before Terra could ask what he was talking about, one of the other men managed to hit her. Terra was surprised at the right hook; she felt pain blossom out from the middle of her torso, and she curled over. Seconds later, as the leader continued to ramble about something, Terra felt her feet swept out from under her.

"Terra!"

She barely heard Davi's cry as he fell to the ground beside her. Terra felt a pounding pain in her head, as she continued to struggle. She felt Davi's arm reach out and protect her, as the last of her consciousness left her.

***

"These two will be perfect for the sacrifice."

Terra felt her eyes try to blink open, but they seemed to be stuck. Remembering what had happened, she decided to make as little movement as she could while she took stock of her situation.

Her head ached, and it felt like her hair was all tangled up in knots. *Did they drag us here?* Terra wondered, before wondering where she was at all.

Carefully and quietly, she shifted her arms against the chill of the cold floor. When she reached out, only a few inches, she immediately felt Davi close to her, his body warm against the surrounding cold. He was knocked out, too, or at least, she was unable to tell if he was awake.

Straining her ears, Terra could suddenly hear her captives as they talked.

"—perfect for the full moon sacrifice. What are you talking about? The girl even has a glow to her skin, so you know she's got to have some good dreams in that pretty little head of hers."

"I don't know, Syras," the other man replied. "Mylan, you can't want to make more trouble for us. It's bad enough that we're already outcasts here on Jewel Island."

"Ha!" Terra recognized Mylan's voice as he scoffed. "Jewel Island was home the Rebel forces all those years ago. It is home to the revolutionary spirit, the one that calls for constant change against the tyranny of tradition. If anything, Aemon and his family have become the outcasts here, and he's managed to drag a good portion of the Islanders along with him."

Terra felt her breath leave her in a rush as she realized where she was all of a sudden. She had been captured, along with Davi, by the Demon Chasers, by the people who believed in Obsidian's power.

And they were going to sacrifice them, under the full moon.

She closed her eyes and grimaced, trying not to let herself feel scared. Her father had taught her to be a Fighter. She could not fail him now, especially with Davi's life on the line as much as hers.

"If the royals are here, wouldn't that explain the glow from the girl, Mylan?"

Terra felt her body go numb again.

"If she is, all the better," Mylan murmured. "Princess Selene was the one who brought Pegasus into this world and managed to seal up Obsidian's power. It is only through the Seal of Blood Sacrifice that we are able to maintain our power now."

The other two men laughed, before Terra heard them leave the room. They were talking to each other, planning for the upcoming sacrifice.

The instant there was nothing but the quiet sound of Davi's breathing, Terra allowed herself to open her eyes. She blinked a few times, trying to displace her pain, and then she saw the room.

The room was dark and cold. She saw she was on the floor in the back room, locked away with Davi. They were not bound up, but they were unable to escape.

Or at least, not escape easily, Terra thought. She studied the room and realized there were several smaller vents. She had been able to overhear a good portion of the Demon Chasers talking from being near the door, too.

She peeked out through under the door. There was no movement, no sound coming from the other rooms. There was very little light, too, she noticed, which made it hard to know just how long they had been in there.

"We must be in their lair," Terra murmured, making mental notes. She continued to make her way around the room, trying to recall other things that Mylan and his friends had said.

They needed a blood sacrifice to keep their power, Terra thought. And they enjoyed finding her, because of her royal blood.

Although they likely did not know about that, Terra reminded herself. It was a mark of a royal to have a certain glow, but since Pegasus had come all those years ago, more people were said to have it, too, thanks to their reclaimed dreams.

"Dreams … " Terra sighed. She did not know how long it had been since they had been on the beach, but she was willing to bet that it was still night. Her family might not know she was missing for another day, and even then, they would be unable to quickly locate her.

And it's not like Davi would have had time to tell anyone about us, either. Terra shook her head at herself. It was possible that, after she'd shamed him earlier at the orphanage, he wouldn't have wanted to tell anyone anyway. He would have wanted her to see he was not scared of her or of what trouble she caused.

Terra wrinkled her nose. "Well, that was a mistake."

"What was a mistake?"

While she had a feeling it was going to be an unpleasant conversation, Terra was relieved to hear Davi stir.

She watched as his eyes opened.. "Going to the beach," she answered, as she helped him sit up.

"I'll say," Davi agreed. He rubbed a hand through his hair. "Any chance you know where we are?"

"Only generally," Terra said. "We're at some kind of house of Demon Chasers. We're locked in their storage room or something, and I have no idea how long we've been gone."

Davi followed her lead at once. "I have a timekeeper on me," he said, pulling out a small device. "It's close to morning."

Terra groaned. "I hope this doesn't mean we'll be stuck here all today," she said.

"Why would we be stuck here all day?"

"The Demon Chasers want to sacrifice us or something, for some kind of ritual," Terra said. "It will likely happen at night, or close to sundown."

"Good point." Davi walked around the small room with her. "Where are they?"

"They're getting things ready, from what I overheard." Terra felt weariness overtake her as she watched him. Davi was one of the few friends she had always been able to count on, even if he was annoying and fretful about things sometimes. And now, it was all her fault that he could die.

As if he could sense her discomfort, he squeezed her hand. "It'll be okay, Terra."

For any number of reasons—she regretted her earlier remarks, she felt guilty for getting him caught up in this, she was secretly relieved that he was with her so she did not have to face this alone—she leaned into him.

"I'm sorry," she whispered, a large lump in her throat.

He held onto her for a long moment, allowing her to embrace him.

Finally, Terra stepped back. She had her tears and her temper under control. Davi's warmth and whispered assurances were able to help her regain her focus.

"Let's get to work," Davi said, and Terra nodded.

Long moments passed as the two of them worked to go over every inch of the room, looking for a weakness, for a way out. They tried pushing through the doors, banging down the vents, and working to find a way to pick or destroy the lock on the door.

Davi sighed as he slumped against the wall. "There's no way out that I can find," he said.

"Maybe we can escape when they come back to get us," Terra said.

"They managed to beat us before."

"So? They had the element of surprise last time," Terra argued. "We won't let them have it again. If anything, we could easily plan it out well enough to where *we* are the ones who surprise them."

Davi reconsidered her plan. "Okay," he agreed. "We should give it a shot, anyway."

"Yeah," Terra said. She yawned. According to Davi's watch, it was still very early in the morning.

"Come here," Davi said, patting the ground beside him.

She never hesitated. She came over and sat down next to him, trying not to think of how little she had eaten at dinner before. He pulled her against him. "Why don't you go to sleep for a bit?" he suggested. "I'll keep watch."

"I don't think I'll be able to sleep now," Terra said, but she leaned against him regardless. "I'm too worried. I mean, our parents might not even know we're gone."

"Carla probably does," Davi said, giving Terra a small smile. "She likes to watch over both of us, you know, even though she's younger than us."

Terra gave him a tepid look. "Maybe. But that might make things worse for us. Or for them. I know how I would feel if either of my parents were lost or hurt or something."

"I know." Davi nodded, and Terra suddenly wondered if he was thinking about that night again.

She sighed. She did not want to think about that. She did not want to think about Tristan or her mother, or her father, or Lem. She did not want to think about Pegasus either, she decided.

"It'll be okay, Terra." Davi rubbed her back comfortingly. "I promise I won't let anything happen to you."

Terra said nothing, keeping her thoughts to herself. Lem had made a promise to her and failed to keep it, and she did not need someone else disappoint him.

Davi kept rubbing her back. She could hear him humming some. She recognized the tune; it was a soft lullaby, one her mother used to sing to her when she was younger.

When she was less fearful—less afraid and less alone.

Terra hated that she felt her eyes drooping shut again, but as sleep took her, she could not find anything worth holding onto in the world around her. Not even Davi's whispered words seemed real enough to grasp onto, as the last of her consciousness once more fell away.

"I love you, Terra. I'll protect you, no matter what. I promise."

***

Terra had no idea how much time had passed before she blinked again, feeling more awake than she had been in a long time. She was surprised when she glanced around and saw that she was back at the beach.

She glanced down at her hands, letting the bright moonlight wash over her palms and glide up her fingers. She could almost feel the warmth of the light, even though she knew it was highly improbable. Up in the sky, she could see both of Sapphira's moons shining with a renewed vigor.

"I told you I would be here when you decided to come back."

Terra nearly jumped at the sound of Lem's voice. She turned around slowly to face him.

She didn't know if she was really surprised or not when she saw him. He was there, barely changed from the last time she had seen him, four years before. He still had the youthful charm on his face, the persistent kindness in his crystal eyes, and the moonlight shimmering off his white hair.

"Lem."

"Terra," he replied. He gave her the same slow, thoughtful smile, the one she had always remembered so clearly. "I have been waiting for you."

"This is a dream," Terra said, and instantly everything made much more sense. That was why Davi had not seen anyone with her, that was why she did not meet him when she went down the Guest House's beachfront. That was why she felt like she missed him, even though it was a one-time encounter.

Lem came up to her. "Of course it is."

"You're not real, then," Terra said. "You've never been real."

"I've *always* been real, Terra," he said patiently. "And I have always been here, waiting for you to come back to the beach."

"I thought you meant the physical beach," Terra murmured apologetically. "If I had known, I might have come to see you sooner."

"Do you really think so?" he asked, his brow arched just enough for her to reconsider how honest she was being.

Terra shrugged, unsure of whether or not to question herself. She would have only come back to see him out of curiosity more than anything else.

But I am back, she suddenly realized. Why had she come back to her dreams? She never allowed herself to dream anymore. She did not *want* to dream anymore. What beauty was there in the world that was worth reliving inside her sleeping mind?

She glanced up at Lem. From the expression on his face, it was as if he was watching her thoughts as they formed and collided with her conscience. "What?" she asked. "What is it?"

"Why don't you tell me?" Lem asked.

"Fine." Terra folded her arms across her chest. "Why are you here? And why are you making me dream again?"

"I'm not here because of anything you did or did not do," Lem told her. "I came at the request of a friend."

"Who?" Terra scoffed. And then she remembered Davi, and remembered how he watched over her. "Ugh, I hope you didn't come for Davi's sake," she grumbled. "He worries too much."

"He worries *for you*."

"He's … " Terra suddenly felt uncomfortable.

"And he wants to protect you," Lem continued. "Just like he wanted to that night we met on the beach."

"We're on the beach now."

He grinned. "The other beach, Terra. The one that you came to, after your brother—"

"No!" Terra shook her head. "I don't want to—"

He did not listen to her. "—after your brother came to live with me."

"What?" Terra stared at him. She had not been expecting him to say *that*. "What are you talking about?" She glared at him, suddenly taking in the whole of who he was.

She faltered. "Who are you?"

"Who do you say I am?" Lem replied, giving her a half-smile. Before she could answer, he laughed. "Your mother was just as surprised, you know."

Terra nearly dropped to her knees in shock. She had not been expecting *that*.

"I guess you are probably more disappointed," Lem remarked, watching her as her gray eyes clouded with a range of wild responses.

Finally, Terra found her ability to speak once more. "She told me that Pegasus was a man. A man with white hair, bronze skin, and crystal-colored eyes … "

She stared at him, still struggling to reconcile what she knew with what she saw. "You're not the right age," she said finally.

Lem shrugged. "I am," he said, "and I have always been. I am the creator of this world, right? Why can't I be any age I want?"

Terra said nothing, too troubled to say anything more. If he was here, and if he was who he said he was, and, if who he said he was was the truth, she thought, there was a good chance that he knew she was likely lying about coming back before.

She had stopped asking questions about Pegasus a long time ago, and she had no right to question him now. After all, she was the one who had left him to wait for her alone on the long beach in her dreams, forgetting him except when she was grieved. He had admitted that she only came to this place now because of Davi's love for her—love she knew she did not deserve.

Lem reached for her hand. "Do you trust me now?" he asked.

She cringed. "Even if I did," Terra said, "I'm not worthy of yours."

"If I am the one who is going to carry you," Lem said, "then it's you that needs to trust me. Either way, you have the right to test me, to make me prove that my word is true."

She had no doubt of his power in that moment. Part of her wanted to say that he was a Demon Chaser, one of the men who had captured her. Maybe even another minion of Mylan's, someone who could reach into her mind and make her dream in illusions and delusions.

But there was something stark about this boy, just as there had been the last time. He was everything she remembered her mother saying, but even more so now, because she could see he was real. She knew if she reached out, she could touch him, and it would be like touching eternity.

She was not unable to see the reality in front of her; she was just reluctant to embrace it.

Terra bit her lip. "You promise you won't hurt me?" she asked.

"Not while we're flying," he replied, giving her a quick grin. The playfulness behind it made her think of her own father.

Finally, Terra tentatively reached for his hand. The instant she took it, there was a flash of power and wind, a sweeping force of music and light. He pulled at her quick and fast, and in a moment she felt herself flying. She did nothing more than blink, and she was suddenly riding through the skies, racing through the clouds and reaching for the stars.

She gasped and looked down, seeing that Lem had transformed into Pegasus, into his Spirit form, and she was riding on his back, heading over the waters of the wide, deep seawaters. Terra grabbed onto his mane tightly as he soared through Sapphira's clouds.

But there was no fear. She was free.

"This is amazing," Terra breathed, unable to process how she was actually asleep and still in her cell. She felt so free and so alive it was hard to think that she was really trapped inside a dark cell, hidden from her family.

As she began mulling over her sudden thoughts, Pegasus swirled down and landed on the beach once more. "I know you're worried," he said. "Tell me what you're thinking."

"Why are the Demon Chasers still here?" Terra asked. "Didn't you rid the world of all the darkness when my mother was younger?"

"I stopped Obsidian's power from preventing people from having good dreams," Pegasus explained. "But there are still many, as you well know, that choose not to dream at all. And there are others, as you also know, who do not dream of beautiful things."

Terra frowned. "Then why don't you make them?" she asked. "I'm here, and not completely of my own choosing, after all."

"Every person still has to be open to choose," Pegasus said. "Davi asked for me to come to you, but I have never left you. You finally came back. And it was more on your own than you would think."

Terra thought about how much she wanted to escape, how she had wanted to find Lem again.

"I guess you're right," Terra said, as she slid off his back. She was glad to see him transform back into his boyish form. Lem's smile was infectious, and it did not seem quite the same coming from Pegasus' form. "So, what do we do now?" she asked. "Will you help me and Davi escape from the Demon Chasers?"

"It has always been one of the greatest wishes for Obsidian to poison the minds of the kings and queens," he replied. "But things have never worked out for them as they would wish. Even when they succeed, they still lose in the end."

"So you're going to help me?" Terra repeated. When he nodded, she frowned. "Why didn't you help my brother, then?"

There was no surprise on Lem's face as she asked that question. His hand reached out and took hold of hers.

"I promise you," he said, "this world, while it has been given a new chance for redemption and healing, is still full of trouble. There will come a time, Terra, when I will make all things new again. But until then, there is still suffering and pain."

"So you let my brother suffer."

"It's not just about you, Terra," Lem said. "It's never been just about one person, even as each person is given the chance."

"Tristan didn't have a chance."

"Your brother had a chance. And he had a beautiful life. And when it was over, he came to live with me in Crystallon."

"What?"

Lem pulled her into a warm embrace, his arm wrapping around her completely. "He lives on, Terra. I have recreated him."

Terra gaped at him, as his words soundly struck her to the very core of her being. The past years of her life demanded to know how, but the childish wonder she had so many years ago seemed to reemerge inside of her.

Her father had said that her brother was in a better place. She had always doubted the truth of that, because he was not with her, not with his family.

But … but what if it was true?

"It's not about you, Terra."

She looked at Lem and felt that same rush of realness. She had never thought of her brother … never thought about him, or what he might have wanted. She had thought about her parents, and what they wanted—or, she realized, what they did not want. She was still more concerned about what she wanted.

And that was just about what she wanted. When she only looked at what she wanted, she often overlooked what was true.

And what was the truth?

She was looking at him.

"I cried with you," Lem admitted, "that day on the beach when I came to meet you. I felt your pain and as you walked away I cried for you. I cried for your mother and your father. But I cheered as your brother came into my home and made his home with me."

Terra found herself at a loss for words again.

"It is no shameful thing to be happy with your life," Lem said. "But there are more important things than your comfort here, Terra. Love is hard, life is unfair, and there will be times when you will have to be brave, especially in its darkest times. I warned your mother, too, but I promised her that I would always be with her. She forgot for a time, but I was there for her when she was ready to come back."

Terra thought about how brave her mother had been just hours earlier, when she had held that baby, Kyrigan, in her arms. She had been denied more children, but she still faced her greatest loss. And her mother always did it with a brave smile.

"I think I get it," Terra told him softly. She felt tears well up in her eyes and spill over.

Lem gave her a somber look. "I might have to remind you again," he warned. "People don't need to be taught so much as they need to be reminded. In your darkness times, I will be there. I have been there. And I am here."

She nodded, before she reached for him. "Help me to hold on, then."

"There's no need for you to worry about holding onto me," Lem said. "I'm holding onto you."

Terra felt the warm wash of his embrace once more as she finally found peace. "Okay."

***

She woke up back in her cell, but still as warm and comforted as she had been on the sand inside of her mind. Terra looked up and saw that, rather than Lem, it was Davi who held her.

He was awake still, staring off into the distance while he held onto her.

For a moment, Terra wondered if everything really had been a dream. Maybe she had dreamed of Lem out of some kind of inner guilt, or maybe she had allowed herself to slip back into her childhood, trying to find any sort of comfort for herself or her family while she was trapped here in the lair of the Demon Chasers.

But even as the old possible explanations came up inside of her mind, Terra knew that there was no real proof. She had experienced it, hadn't she? She knew it was real. She knew it was right.

"Davi," she whispered. She could feel his wince at her words.

"Are you okay, Terra?" he asked. The tired concern in his voice made her feel even more terrible for the things she had told him earlier. "I didn't wake you, did I?"

"No," she assured him. "No. If anything, you helped me sleep as well as I did." She did not want to tell him about Pegasus. Terra felt that, even though Davi was a true friend, she did not want to share with him how much she felt humbled. He would still enjoy it too much for comfort, she silently decided.

Davi shifted underneath her again. "I guess it would be hard to fall asleep here, to wonder if you were going to die, and then to wait for it."

Terra said nothing. She could tell that he was still struggling with his own fear, but he still sought to ease hers.

While she did not usually admire Davi for his courage, she knew that courage was at its truest when faced with the greatest fear.

She slid off his shoulder before she slipped into his arms in a tight hug. He was even more surprised than she was as she reached up and kissed his cheek softly. "Thank you," she whispered.

Several long moments passed before he responded. "You're welcome."

Terra thought about pointing out that he was getting a chance to be her bodyguard at last, but she decided it was better to hold onto him and say nothing.

***

The Demon Chasers did not come back until after several more hours passed. Terra was beginning to wonder if they were going to be left in the small room, left to die of starvation and thirst.

During that time, she and Davi talked quietly together, trying to form a plan of escape. They tried to force open the door, to squeeze out the vents, and to call for help. But there was no answer.

When they were calling through the vents, the Demon Chasers came back. They were not pleased to hear their captives.

Mylan and Syras, and other supporters, came into the room and stopped them.

"Ouch," Davi cried, unable to stop himself from yelping in pain.

"Oh, do stop," Syras grumbled, as he slammed Davi against the wall once more.

"Leave us alone," Terra shouted, as Mylan began to bind her hands with some rope. "We are nothing but trouble for you."

"That's for sure," Mylan muttered, as he tugged hard on the knot. Terra grimaced at the rope's worn bristles as they sliced into her skin. "But I am hoping that your blood will be well worth it in the end."

"It's your blood that I would be more concerned about," Terra snapped.

Mylan cocked an eyebrow. "Do you need a gag, too?" He grinned as he pulled out a knife and tossed it to Syras. "Maybe that will work even better?"

Terra narrowed her gaze as Syras pushed the tip of the knife into Davi's neck. She relented at once; she did not want them to hurt Davi, and especially because of her insolence. "Fine," she snapped. "But you better not hurt him."

"Don't give me a reason," Mylan shot back. "Now, let's go. The tides are low, and it is time we headed to the altar."

"Terra," Davi whispered. "Please, it's alright. We'll be alright."

Syras laughed as he secured Davi's hands. "That's right," he agreed, as he guffawed with laughter. "Everything always turns out right when you're dead."

Terra thought about what Lem had told her. Was it possible that she would have to face death?

She thought about Tristan. He had faced death, and death had won. Was it her turn?

No, she thought. *No, wait. That's not true. Lem told me that Tristan is with the Guardian of Dreams, in Crystallon.*

She felt a new wave of tears. Death had not won against her brother, even though he faced it; he passed through it, and now he was safe.

He was safe, and he was waiting for her.

Terra straightened her shoulders. If this was the end, it was only the end of one part of her life. She would face death bravely. She glanced back at Davi, trying to show him she was not afraid.

And she wasn't. She thought about Lem, about how he had been with her all these years as she was consumed with her own pain. Maybe he had come to her in the last moments of her life to save her from her own despair. Maybe he had come to show her there was a better life out there for her, outside of her pain and inner angst. Maybe he loved her and wanted her to be a better person, even if it was for only a few moments. Maybe he wanted to show her that he was with her, so she would look to him as she was swept up out of the mortal plane.

Davi looked over at her and caught her eye. Terra, knowing him as well as she did after all these years, could see that he was clearly worried only for her, and not for himself. Terra made a silent promise to herself that she would ask her father if Davi would be assigned to be her Protector.

***

Terra briefly recalled Mylan talking about a full moon sacrifice as they walked along the rocky path. While Terra was not completely sure where they were, she knew that they were climbing down into a niche on the mountain, heading down into the heart of darkness.

She was glad, as she struggled not to stumble on the many pointed rocks and the slippery mounds of dirt, that she had worn her shoes out to the beach before.

Davi shuffled behind her. His hands were bound behind his back, just as hers were. Terra managed to get a few glimpses of the surrounding area, hoping to find someone around that would realize Mylan was up to no good.

Mylan and his crew walked alongside them, keeping them moving forward, talking of the full moon ritual they were about to carry out. Terra shuddered at the thought of being a blood sacrifice. At that terrifying thought, Terra momentarily lost her confidence and her courage. She stumbled and scraped her knee against the ground.

"Ouch," she muttered, trying to keep her voice low. She saw Syras' smirk as he held onto Davi's arm.

"Whoa, no need offer up your blood until we're ready," one of Mylan's other henchmen joked, stirring up a round of laughter from the others.

"Are you alright?" Davi whispered as he scuttled closer to her.

"I'm fine," she said, and she tried to make it a promise.

They headed deeper into the mountain, before they came to a small cave. There was a high slant in the ceiling, and Terra saw a large beam of light pouring in from the outside.

Even though it was dark out, she was still able to see a lot, she realized. She thought of the previous night, where she had seen Shira and Kuro's light. She had thought nothing of it at the time, but they were waxing brightly in the Sapphiran horizon.

The rest of the light, coming in from the sun behind her, was shut out as one of the men pulled a curtain over the opening of the cave.

Mylan brought Terra and Davi to a halt before a large stone altar. Terra felt queasy, looking at its smooth, gray surface. She felt the last of her hope leave her as she and Davi were forced to sit down on it.

While she watched, the men gathered up bundles of sticks and peat. Terra knew at once what was going to happen. She and Davi would be killed, sacrificed so the men could keep the power of darkness alive in their own hearts. And then they would burn them, so the smell of blood would waft to the Four-Point Celestial Prison, the one in which Obsidian was bound.

"Terra … " Davi's voice was quiet, but she thought she could hear it shake.

"What is it?" she whispered back.

"I'm … I'm not sure if we'll be able to fight them," Davi admitted.

"We can try," Terra said, but feeling her own bonds, she wondered if Davi had a point.

But he seemed to instantly brighten. "You're right," he said. "Even if there is no hope now, we can wait for it to come. And then we can try something."

Terra nodded. "I'm sorry I said you were a coward," she told him. "I don't think you are, not really. And especially not now."

"For all the good it does," Davi replied.

"No," Terra said, shaking her head. "It does a lot of good. I promise. If I am going to die here, I'm glad it is with you."

He caught his eyes with hers, and Terra felt taken aback. She had watched Davi grow up as she did, but it was not until that moment that she finally seemed to see him as he was. Some part of her started to wonder how their lives would be if they survived, but no part of her ever considered that it would be without him.

A glint of light beamed into her eye, and Terra turned to see Mylan had once more claimed his knife from Syras.

"Now, my blood brothers," he intoned, "it is time to begin!"

Terra shuddered and leaned against Davi. She hoped the men would allow her that small comfort, of feeling the warmth of her best friend before the fires of blood and sacrifice strangled the life from her.

As the men began to chant, and the seconds before her death sharpened, Terra's only thoughts turned to her time with Pegasus—Lem—and how she would be with her brother soon.

Despite everything, Terra felt herself smile, even as tears ran down her cheeks.

"And now, Lord Obsidian," Mylan cried, waving the knife around in the moonlight as he was surrounded by the others, carrying torches of their own, "we offer these dreamers to you. May their blood wash away any remnant of light we have within us!"

Terra squeezed her eyes shut and pressed into Davi even more.

But before the blade of the knife could strike her, moonlight came pouring into the cave, striking down on the altar.

Mylan suddenly gasped in pain, and Terra heard a familiar voice call out, "Stop!"

She dared herself to peek up at what was happening. Terra gaped up at the stream of moonlight as it flooded her vision. Mylan dropped the knife, which was now smoking. He fell to his knees, grasping at his hand. Terra saw that it was burning, too, as if the light was eating at his flesh.

Davi nudged her from behind. "Terra," he hissed. "We can make our escape! Let's go."

Before Terra could agree, the curtain of the cave was pulled back, and the shadow of her father came bursting into the room. Several others came in after him; some were their guards, while some came bearing the crest of Jewel Island. Terra was surprised to see her Uncle Aemon there as well, helping her father fight off the Demon Chasers.

Davi managed to free himself and then turned to work on her bonds.

As the last of the ropes fell from her wrists, Terra felt herself swept up in her father's embrace.

"Terra!" Etoileon crushed her to him, cradling her in his arms. "I was so worried for you."

"Daddy," Terra whimpered, so relieved to realize she would live. All her bravado melted as she watched her father struggle not to cry, and fail as he held onto her. For a moment, Terra wondered if she should be the one who comforted him.

"How did you find us?" Terra asked. "We haven't seen anyone for hours."

"Your mother heard from an old friend of hers," he said with a knowing smile. "And a new one of yours, apparently."

Lem.

Terra thought about what he had said to her before. Her hands went numb, as his word proved to be true in the end. He was who he said he was—and she knew it. He had saved her, and Davi, in the end.

Terra was distracted from her inner awe as her father kissed her forehead. "I love you," he told her. "I was so worried, and so was your mother."

"Is she here too?" Terra asked, craning her neck to see if she could spot the familiar figure of her mom.

"No," Etoileon said. He gave her a shaky laugh. "I wouldn't let her come. She was very distraught. Davi's mother is with her. She felt the same way, so they are back at the house tending to each other."

"My mom is okay?" Davi asked.

Etoileon opened his arms to him. "Yes," he said, embracing the both of them. "Everyone is okay."

Davi reached his arm around Terra. "I guess everything turned out alright in the end after all, Terra."

She smiled. "Yes, it did."

***

Everything was alright in the end, but it took several days for Terra to process everything that happened. When she arrived back at the Guest House, she embraced her mother for a long time, feeling a new sense of fervency and desperation between them.

Terra felt no greater joy than when her mother and father came and held her between them, kissing her cheeks and caressing her hair.

"I love you," she told them, and she knew she had never meant it more.

Her mother, gracious as always, smiled brightly. "We love you so much, Terra. No one could ever take your place."

"We will always love you," her father added. "And we will always protect you as much as we can."

At his words, Terra thought of that night when her father had admitted he felt like a failure after Tristan had died. As she walked through the Guest House in the following days, she knew he was watching for her. Terra knew that he was afraid that he had nearly failed again, but she knew that her father was a true hero.

Later that week, Terra learned from Aemon that the Demon Chasers had been hiding out for several months; other Islands had complained of them. The Demon Chasers had several locations where they would move throughout the year.

"Did you get them all when you came to free me?" Terra asked her uncle as he sat down to dinner with them. She could not help but notice that since the rescue, she was seeing more of her uncle and his family. Tensions between the families had dispersed. She knew that there was a long history between them, so Terra was glad that, if nothing else, her extended family was gradually coming together.

Aemon sighed and shrugged. "Not likely," he muttered, and even Selene frowned at his tone. He sighed at the reaction and said, "There are several small groups of these Demon Chasers. We caught all of the ones that were here, but it remains to be seen if there are more groups that will come this way."

"I hope not," Selene said. "I know they seek out places like this for reasons."

Davi leaned over and whispered to Terra, "She means because of the orphanages," he said. "I overheard your dad say they like to use children for their dark deeds."

Terra nodded. "I wondered as much," she admitted, thinking of the strange feeling she had felt at her mother's charity.

Davi reached over and took her hand affectionately, offering his own silent comfort. Terra gave him a smile in return, even though she had to wonder if she needed his comfort at all.

In the last week, she had seen some of the darkness things that life had to offer, but she still had hope—and she no longer had to wonder if it was possible that beautiful things could come from terrible things.

Her dreams had returned. While it seemed rocky and awkward to be back in the lands of her childhood, juxtaposed against the darkness of her realities, Terra knew that it was just part of the truth of her life—that there was a deep overlapping of worlds inside of her, ones of pain and pleasure, providence and purpose. She knew it was her duty and privilege to walk among those worlds with steady steps, just as she knew that she would have someone to carry her when her feet failed her.

In the end, she squeezed Davi's hand in return. He loved her enough to offer her comfort, and she was honored by that. So she took it and cherished it, and promised never to take him for granted again.

As the dinner continued, Terra glanced out one of the windows, looking down toward the beach.

She was surprised to see Lem there, waving at her from the waterfront. When she lifted a hand to wave back, he bowed deeply before transforming back into Pegasus.

Terra smiled brightly as the winged horse dashed across the sky like lightning, before diving deeply into a sea of moonlight.

C. S. Johnson is the author of several young adult novels, including sci-fi and fantasy adventures such as *The Starlight Chronicles* series, the *Once Upon a Princess* saga, and the *Divine Space Pirates* trilogy. With a gift for sarcasm and an apologetic heart, she currently lives in Atlanta with her family.

AUTHOR'S NOTE AND ACKNOWLEDGEMENTS

Dear Reader,

Over the years, I'll admit that I've tried to ignore *The Moonlight Pegasus*. It was an early, early attempt at writing, something I wrote while I was desperately lonely and insecure in high school. It was published a couple of months before I graduated. Reading through it now, ten years after its original publication, I am forced to confront an uncomfortable truth about myself: I was not always as confident nor as correct about the world as I thought I was.

Still, I am happy to see some of the more girlish elements that remain. When I see them, I feel almost like I am walking by the metaphorical landmarks as I journey further into the mind of my younger self. I can clearly see my love for God, and the young urgency of my devotion to him—more of a "first love" variety, rather than the more "seasoned beloved" that I am now. My ardent love of poetry and nature, the unbounded idealism, and the quest for beauty, truth, and goodness are all there, running through the story like blood beating through a heart.

After I graduated high school, I started writing what would become *The Starlight Chronicles*. The tone of these two projects is almost, no pun intended, night and day. Selene is a lonely, lovely girl who faces great sadness; Hamilton is a spoiled, narcissistic teenager who is uncomfortable with the idea of personal responsibility and sacrifice. After I finished *The Moonlight Pegasus*, some part of my idealism died as I faced high school's lingering shadow, and college's hard-hitting realism. And I, as C. S. Lewis put it, "put childish things behind me," and moved on from *Pegasus*.

Over the years, I have had a few fans write to me, asking if I was going to do a sequel. I did not really feel like a sequel was warranted, so I always said the same thing: No, but if I did, I would write about Selene and Etoileon's daughter, Terra. As I wrote the ending, I knew they would go on and have a family, and raise their children in love, and true to my idealism, everything would be perfect—and it's hard to write a story when there is no conflict.

Realism strikes again, this time in the form of my own children. Ten years later, I realize more fully the struggles and surprises, the triumphs and trials, the work and play of parenting. And I know now what kind of troubles come, even for perfectly loving families. Most of the ones that inspired this story revolve around legacy.

How do I pass along the good things of my life, the things that have defined my life, to my children?

I struggle with the idea of sharing God with my kids. I do what I can, but my kids will never walk through the valley I crawled through in high school. They will never completely feel my isolation and despair—of course, they will have their own, should life have its way. But they will never experience my life through my eyes, and because of this, I worry they will never understand the reasons or the rhymes behind my beliefs, and everything that subsequently follows.

And subsequently, *everything* follows from there.

That's a terrifying thought, especially when I think it. We take it for granted what we have, thanks to those who have come before us. I know a favorite author of mine, Amy Tan, has written on this too, about the struggles of passing on a heritage and family history when there seems to be such distance—mentally, physically, emotionally—between people, even people who are standing close together in history's moments.

I likened it to a friend as trying to capture how the children of Israel felt, a generation after Moses led them through the Red Sea. How would you feel? I would wonder if it was real, if it was really what people thought it was, if people were not just trying to live in the past or in better times, or if it was something that continued to haunt the previous generation.

So that's how Terra's story was born.

It was an unexpected surprise to me, and not all an unwelcome one. But I hope you have enjoyed it as much as I hoped you would, and I also hope you continue to check out my other work, too, as varied and unexpected as some of those other adventures and questions may seem.

Until We Meet Again,

C. S. Johnson

88

Thank you for reading! Please leave a review for this book
and check for other books and updates!